The Chronicles of Narnia®, Narnia®, and all book titles, characters and locales original to The Chronicles of Narnia
are trademarks of C.S. Lewis Pte. Ltd. Use without permission is strictly prohibited.

Published in Great Britain by HarperCollins Children's Books, a division of HarperCollins*Publishers,*
77-85 Fulham Palace Road, Hammersmith, London W6 8JB
A CIP catalogue for this title is available from the British Library.

The HarperCollins Children's Books website address is: www.harpercollinschildrensbooks.co.uk

ISBN 0-00-716292-8

❖

3 5 7 9 10 8 6 4 2

The Lion, the Witch and the Wardrobe
Copyright © 2004 by C.S. Lewis Pte. Ltd. Text adapted from *The Lion, the Witch and the Wardrobe,*
copyright © 1950 by C.S. Lewis Pte. Ltd.
Artwork by Tudor Humphries; copyright © 2004 by C.S. Lewis Pte. Ltd.

Printed in China for Imago All rights reserved.
The Narnia website address is: www.narnia.com

THE LION, THE WITCH AND THE WARDROBE

BASED ON THE ORIGINAL BOOK BY

C. S. Lewis

Retold by Hiawyn Oram

Illustrated by Tudor Humphries

Collins

An imprint of HarperCollinsPublishers

Once there was – and probably still is – a magic wardrobe.

It was made from the wood of a magic apple tree, and you could, if you would, climb through the back to another world . . . to a magical land called Narnia.

But now that world was ruled by an icy White Witch, whose wand could turn you to stone and whose power could be broken only with the help of four children.

And of course, right here on this side of the wardrobe, were four children . . . Peter, Susan, Edmund and Lucy . . . all of them longing for adventure.

Lucy, the youngest, and most longing, was first to push past the furry coats . . .

and find herself in a snowy wood, under a streetlamp . . .
where the Witch's wickedness had made it always winter.

"Always winter and never Christmas . . . imagine that!" came a voice. It was Mr Tumnus, a faun. He was working for the Witch, even though he knew it was wrong. "Good evening!" he said, staring hard at Lucy. "You *are* a human child, are you not? Come through the wild west woods?"

"No!" said Lucy. "Through the wardrobe in the spare room!"

"War Drobe? Spare Oom? Never heard of them!" said Mr Tumnus. "But someone like you is expected, and a toasty tea awaits you. . . ."

After tea, to Lucy's surprise, Mr Tumnus began to weep so hard that there were puddles all over the floor. Lucy had often wanted to cry like that herself and was most sympathetic, which made Mr Tumnus blurt out the truth.

"I'm supposed to hand you over to Her Wicked White Majesty, but now that I've met you, I can't, I won't! Even though I'll be turned to stone if I don't!"

Lucy promised she wouldn't let that happen. "After all," she said, "a witch is only a witch until someone stands up to her in the right way. So, I'll get my brothers and sister and that's what we'll do!"

But before Lucy could persuade Peter and Susan that there *was* a wicked White Witch through the wardrobe, Edmund secretly slipped through to see for himself . . .

and bumped straight into her!

At once the Witch saw he was just the
kind of boy she could win over with a box
of her enchanted Turkish Delight. "And
there'll be lots more . . . rooms full of it,"
she tempted him, "if you'll only bring
your brother and sisters to my House!"

"I will, I will," said Edmund, stuffing
and gobbling, without stopping to think
what might happen to them if he did.

"Then I'll make you a King." That
beautiful, wickeder-than-wicked Witch
smiled.

So when, a few days later, all four children *did* go through the wardrobe together, Edmund was quite ready to deliver the others to the Witch . . . just to get his mouth around more of that magic, must-have Turkish Delight.

Of course, he said nothing as they trudged through the snow in coats borrowed from the wardrobe.

He said nothing when they found Mr Tumnus's cave ransacked.

He said not a word when a Talking Beaver told them Mr Tumnus had been dragged away by the Witch's Secret Wolf Police.

Lucy, on the other hand, was furious. "Well, that does it," she cried. "I'm not leaving until that Witch has had her wand smashed and her wickedness stamped on!"

Mr Beaver was thrilled to hear Lucy talk like this and hurried them back to his house for a what-to-do-about-the-witch meeting.

"You have come at exactly the right time," said Mrs Beaver.

"You have, indeed," said Mr Beaver. "For it is well known that to get rid of the Witch, Aslan needs four brave and adventurous children!"

"Aslan?" cried Lucy with a shiver of excitement. "Who is Aslan?"

"Aslan the Great, of course," said Mr Beaver, "who created this world and all of us in it . . . the only one more powerful than the Witch."

"And" – Mrs Beaver gathered them closer – "they say he will be at the Stone Table by tomorrow. But *sshh* . . . the Witch mustn't hear of it, and her spies are everywhere."

They were soon so busy whispering about meeting Aslan, they did not notice Edmund sneaking out the back . . .

to make his way to the Witch's House and more Turkish Delight!

But nothing could have prepared him for what he found when he got there: every kind of creature turned to stone; air so cold it was frosted white; the Witch's Wolf Captain stretched out, smirking; and the Witch in the foulest mood, hating him on sight.

"Where are your sisters and brother?" she snapped, her breath forming icicles.

"I'll g-g-get them to you," Edmund managed to say through chattering teeth. "R-r-right n-now . . . they're going to the Stone to m-meet someone called A-a-as . . . ?"

"ASLAN? I knew it! No wonder the temperature's rising in here! LONGBEARD! My sleigh! ASLAN AND THOSE CHILDREN MUST NOT REACH EACH OTHER!"

But, keeping to hidden paths and deep forest, the Beavers were already leading Lucy, Peter and Susan to meet Aslan.

"Sleigh bells!" cried Lucy suddenly. "Quick, hide! It might be *Her*!"

"No! Look!" said Mr Beaver. "It must be a sign from Aslan!"

Lucy looked and her heart leaped. Father Christmas was here!

He was not like any Father Christmas she'd ever heard of or seen – nor were his gifts.

"I bring you what your adventures call for," he said mysteriously. Lucy held hers carefully. It was a small diamond bottle of cordial made from fireflowers, so magical that a few drops would heal the wounded.

At the thought of the wounded, Lucy remembered Edmund. She had the feeling something terrible was happening to him . . .

and it was.

The Witch had him tied like a
prisoner . . . and was raging at him
as if it was *his* fault her winter was
wearing out, her sledge wasn't working
and that, everywhere, there were signs
of spring.

But deep down she knew it was
Aslan's doing, and she knew the
prophecy. "The day Aslan crowns four
children Kings and Queens of Narnia,
my rule will end! Except it won't," she
snarled at her lurking Wolf Captain.
"I'll defeat him yet! Go get the other
three while I decide how best to use
this fool of a boy!"

But defeating Aslan would never be
that simple . . . even for the White
Witch.

As Lucy and Peter and Susan were discovering at the Table, Aslan was
nobler than any creature imaginable.

He was a lion, greater than all lions, and wonderful and terrible at the
same time. For Lucy, looking at him felt like looking at the sun, only safer.

When Aslan spoke, his deep, rich voice seemed to shake the very ground Lucy stood on.

"Welcome, children! Long have we waited for you. . . ."

He turned to the horizon. "There in that castle are four thrones. Only when four human children occupy them will Narnia be free again. But crowns must be earned, and that time is upon you. . . ."

At this, there was great consternation among the smaller Narnians. Peter and the Beavers ran to see what it was all about. But Lucy felt she had to tell Aslan about Edmund.

"He is lost, Aslan!" she began. And then the words tumbled out. "Or with the Witch, or taken by the Witch. Or something. But please, he *is* our brother! And he is the *fourth*. He must be saved!"

"All shall be done that must be," said Aslan, "all dealt with in turn and first—"

He was interrupted by the sound of the horn Father Christmas had given Susan. She was giving warning that the Witch's Wolf Captain was slinking towards them.

Lucy was up a tree in a flash, but Susan hadn't time to climb out of reach. "Help her!" Lucy screamed.

And drawing his sword, Peter did . . . fighting that lurking, smirking, cruel Captain single-handedly, to his end.

"You are finding your strengths, I see." Aslan glowed. "And now, I must send my people for your brother."

True to Aslan's promise, in the morning, Edmund had been found. He was there . . . walking in the dewy grass and talking with the Lion. Lucy thought her brother looked quite different . . . as if he was beginning to trust himself again. She was so relieved she wanted to run over and throw her arms around him, but before she could, the dwarf, Longbeard, announced the arrival of the White Witch.

"Hear me!" the Witch screamed at Aslan. "That child was ready to hand over his brother and sisters in exchange for a few boxes of Turkish Delight. He is a traitor! And cannot be rescued. For the Law says all traitors are mine. Give him back to me NOW!"

When she had finished, Aslan sent Peter to prepare an army of good Narnians. Then he quietly offered his own life to save Edmund's.

The Witch couldn't believe her luck! "Forget Edmund," she whispered to her dwarf and her hags. "Forget the children! Now I can kill the great Aslan, Power of All Good, without breath or roar . . . and rule forever! Tie him to the Table with a thousand ropes!"

But as soon as Aslan was dead and the Witch left, an army of mice arrived and began to nibble through the ropes. Lucy and Susan, who had been hidden, were heartbroken. They wanted to run and tell Peter, but before they could, there came a thunderous crack.

The Stone Table had split in two – and Aslan was free.

"Aslan! You're alive!" Lucy cried, flinging herself onto him. "How did you do that?"

"Through Magic deeper than the Witch will ever know," said Aslan. "And now, children, there is much to do . . . but first we shall enjoy a romp through spring as no one ever has, except in Narnia."

And that is what they did, the girls riding on the great Lion's back, through avenues and sunny glades, past roaring waterfalls and echoing caverns, across mountains, valleys and acres of blue flowers . . .

on and on . . . until they arrived at the Witch's House. She was away, of course, but high walls and locked gates did not bother Aslan. "Hold on!" he roared, and leaped . . . and landed in the courtyard . . . among statues of all the creatures the Witch had turned to stone.

"Mr Tumnus!" cried Lucy. "Oh, Aslan, I promised him I wouldn't let this happen!"

"Then keep your promise through me," said Aslan as he began to breathe warm life into each of the cold statues. And, once back in the land of the living, all of them were only too eager to join in the battle against the Witch . . .

and her horrible army of ogres and giants, boggles and hags, ghouls and ghastlies of every sort.

But as they came bounding up, they saw stone statues of *their* side, all over the battlefield. The Witch and her wand were winning! Then, suddenly, Edmund stepped out to save the day. Instead of going for the Witch directly, he brought his sword down on her wand . . . smashing it to pieces!

"Fools! All of you!" the Witch screeched, turning on Peter. "I'll still find a way!"

Peter staggered back . . . and Aslan made his greatest leap yet, straight at the Witch.

And that was that. "The White Witch is dead! Narnia is free! Long live Narnia!" The cries went up, sending the last of the Witch's army running for the faraway hills.

As Edmund lay still on the ground, Lucy remembered her fireflower cordial and rushed to his side.

"He's badly wounded," said Peter, "but without what he did, the Witch would have won."

"True," said Aslan, "even I might be a statue. He has earned his place back among you. But, Lucy, be quick. There are many wounded. Susan, help her while I get busy with all these statues!"

When every hurt Narnian was healed and every stone statue was breathing again, Aslan solemnly crowned the children up at the castle: King Peter, Queen Susan, King Edmund and Queen Lucy.

Afterwards there was music, feasting and dancing. Aslan, glowing more golden than ever, was about to slip away. But before he did, Lucy found him.

"We've never ruled anywhere before," she said. "And . . . I am a bit afraid."

"Don't be," said Aslan. "For I'll be with you, even when you do not see me. Besides, you're all brave and adventurous, and I've seen the love in your heart, Lucy, and it overflows. You will be as good a queen as Narnia could hope for."

As always, Aslan was right. Soon all four of them were loved and respected up and down the land. Together, they finished off the Witch's ghastlies. They restored peace, good living and laughter, and where once it was endless winter, now it seemed always summer.

"The Prophecy is fulfilled," said Mr Tumnus, as they walked in the wild woods.

"Narnia is Narnia again. But, what's this? An iron tree, lit like a lamp?"

Of course, it wasn't an iron tree at all. It was the lamppost near the wardrobe!

Suddenly, Peter, Susan, Edmund and Lucy felt the pull of their lives on the other side. And the next thing . . . there they were . . . not pushing past trees . . . but rows of fur coats!

They were back! They were home! And, to their amazement, not a moment had passed since they'd left. But then, as they were to find out in many other adventures, that was all part of the marvel and mystery of that evermore magical land . . . Narnia!